Nettlepatch Farm

PERCY THE DUCK

Abigail Pizer

MACMILLAN CHILDREN'S BOOKS

First published 1988 by
MACMILLAN CHILDREN'S BOOKS
A division of Macmillan Publishers Limited
London and Basingstoke
Associated companies throughout the world

British Library Cataloguing in Publication Data
Pizer, Abigail
  Percy the Duck. — (Nettlepatch Farm series).
  I. Title II. Series
  823'. 914 [J]   PZ7

  ISBN 0-333-44736-0

Printed in Hong Kong

It is autumn at Nettlepatch Farm.
On the farm live Mr Potter, Mrs Potter and
their little daughter Amy.

The leaves have turned a golden brown and
have begun to fall from the trees.
When the sun shines it is no longer hot.
Often it rains.

Most of the animals on the farm are glad to
be out of the rain.
But the ducks love it.
They swim on the pond and they play in the
mud.
All except Percy.

Every day Percy watches the wild ducks come flying into the pond.

At the end of the day he watches them fly
away, high into the sky.
And that is what Percy wants to do – to fly.

Percy is determined to fly.
There must be a way of learning.

And Percy waddles off to the end of the farmyard.

He turns round, takes a deep breath, and
begins to run as fast as his legs will let him.

He flaps his wings, harder and harder, he
runs and runs . . .

. . . and crashes straight into a pile of old tyres.

Percy gives his feathers a
good shake to get them
straight again.

Percy looks at the old shed by the barn.
He looks at the planks piled up against the side.

Percy scrambles up the planks.
He gets on to the roof, flaps his wings as hard as he can, and . . .

. . . down he goes into the water trough!

Percy is sure that his next idea will work.
He waddles up a pile of straw bales.

When he reaches the top he starts to run
very quickly towards the edge.
He jumps off, flapping his wings – but then
he falls and falls . . .

. . . and lands with a plop in a pool of mud!

But still Percy is not put off.
The only reason why he can't get off the
ground or stay in the sky is now plain
to him.
He is too heavy.

It is Amy's job to look after the ducks.
She sees that Percy is not eating. He won't
eat the duck feed, he won't eat the kitchen
scraps. Amy even tempts him with some cat
food.
But Percy will not eat a thing.

Amy is worried about Percy, so she watches
him.
She sees him looking at the wild ducks each
evening.
She suddenly realises why Percy is
unhappy.

Amy tells her father. Mr Potter says that Percy is too young
to fly now, but in a few weeks he should be able to fly a
little way.

In the meantime, Percy keeps trying . . . and trying.

Until one day he flies!
Not very far, or very high, but he flies.

Percy is so pleased and proud.
He has taught himself to fly.

Nettlepatch Farm